The
GHOST
GARDEN

First published in 2021 in Great Britain by
Barrington Stoke Ltd
18 Walker Street, Edinburgh, EH3 7LP

www.barringtonstoke.co.uk

A CIP catalogue record for this book is available
from the British Library upon request

ISBN: 978-1-78112-900-5

Printed by Hussar Books, Poland

Emma Carroll

With illustrations by
Kaja Kajfež

Barrington Stoke

Chapter 1

Fran found the bone in the potato patch. It was lying deep in the soil, as dark as an old tree root. The prong of Fran's garden fork hit it with a grim *thwack*.

"Oh!" Fran said as she leapt back, startled. She crouched down for a better look.

Much to Fran's disappointment, there was no skeleton attached to the bone. No skull baring its teeth. It was just a single bone – so big that it might have once been a creature's leg, Fran guessed. She'd broken it with her fork. A fresh, jagged line ran right along the length of it as it lay gleaming in the dirt.

Fran sat back on her heels. She felt guilty now, as if she'd hurt some real living thing. She glanced behind her to check her father hadn't noticed what had happened. He was still bent over a row of lettuces, deciding which ones to pull for lunch.

Fran's father was Head Gardener here at Longbarrow House, which was owned by old Mrs Walker. He'd taken the job two years ago, and Fran loved working alongside him during her school holidays. Often she'd find lost objects in the house's vast gardens – clay pipes, bits of china, a pretty hat pin, a shilling piece. But Fran had never found a bone before. And this one was disturbingly human-sized.

Fran shivered despite the heat of the summer morning. Where had the bone come from? Ideas rushed into her head as she wiped her hands on her pinafore and got to her feet: murder, kidnap, a missing person. Fran moved fast to cover the bone over again with soil before anyone else saw it.

"You done digging spuds?" her father called.

Fran pointed to the basket on the ground beside her. "That's got to be enough, hasn't it?" she replied.

The potatoes and the lettuces were for Mrs Walker and her grandchildren. For most of the year, her grandchildren went away to school somewhere strict and expensive. But they came to Longbarrow House for the summer because their parents were always working. Their father – Mrs Walker's son – was an officer in the army. Their mother was a writer who lived in Paris.

At first, everyone had thought Fran would be dying to make friends with the grandchildren: she was an only child, after all. Yet Fran had always preferred her own company or that of adults. Mrs Walker was a kind, clever lady who shared Fran's love of mystery stories. The Walker grandchildren, however, were the noisiest, silliest, *hungriest* children Fran had ever met. She could hardly believe they were related to Mrs Walker.

*

Fran picked up the basket of potatoes and walked briskly towards the house with it on her hip. She enjoyed this part of the day, already thinking about the plate of delicious butter biscuits Millie would have waiting for her. Millie worked in the kitchens and was one of the few people Fran trusted and liked. Millie had a soft Irish voice and smiling eyes, and always gushed over the fine produce Fran's father grew.

Fran heard Mrs Walker's grandchildren before she saw them. They were on the far side of the enormous front lawn. Fran guessed they were playing cricket – from the squeals and the *tock* of a bat hitting a ball. With her head down, she kept walking, hoping they wouldn't spot her.

The Walkers had arrived the last week of June in a motorcar piled high with luggage. Leo, Evan and Jessie were handsome, healthy children with spotless white clothes and neat hair. Last summer, Fran tried to be friendly towards them, after her parents nagged her.

But every attempt to speak to the Walker children left Fran feeling tongue-tied and stupid. Leo, the eldest, wouldn't even look at her. But the twins, Evan and Jessie, mimicked Fran's country accent and laughed at the dirt under her fingernails.

"You can play with us," Jessie had said. "But please don't touch our clothes."

This year Fran had already decided to keep out of their way. If this was what brothers and sisters were like, Fran was glad to have none of her own.

She heard a yell from the other side of the lawn and saw a small figure in white hurtling towards her. Fran walked even faster.

"I say, Frannie!" called Evan. "Hold on there!"

Fran hated that he called her that, but the panic in Evan Walker's voice made her glance round. He stopped in front of her, his cricket whites smeared with what looked worryingly like blood.

"We need your help," cried Evan. "It's my brother." He waved towards the far end of the lawn, where someone now lay flat on the grass.

Fran hesitated, thinking it might be a joke.

"It's Leo's leg," Evan explained. "Jessie walloped him with the bat."

Fran frowned.

"She didn't mean to hit him so hard," Evan added hastily, "but he was being a bit of a plank. Going on and on about some duke being shot in Europe and how—"

"How bad is it?" Fran interrupted Evan. She didn't have time to hear Leo's thoughts about the world or Evan's explanation of them.

"Something's sticking out of his trouser leg," Evan said. "It looks like bone."

A picture of it flew into Fran's head all too fast: jagged, creamy-white. Fran flinched, remembering hitting the bone she'd found in the potato patch. It took a lot of force to break something like that.

Fran put down the vegetable basket, pretty sure now that Evan wasn't joking. "You'd better show me," she said.

She followed Evan across the grass, determined to be brave. But Leo Walker's leg was worse than she'd expected, and the sight of it made Fran dizzy. Leo's trousers were torn just below the knee. The rip revealed the splintered end of a leg bone. There was blood on the cricket bat, the grass, Jessie's summer dress. Leo was groaning in agony.

Fran felt sick with panic. They needed to get Leo back to the house as fast as they could. Mrs Walker would know what to do next.

"We'll have to lift him together," Fran told the twins.

But they couldn't look at Leo without sobbing. It was useless.

"He's going to die!" Evan cried.

"It's all my fault!" Jessie wailed.

Yes, Fran thought as she gritted her teeth. *It* is *your fault, Jessie, you nasty little girl.*

Then Millie and Fran's father came running, and soon Leo was safely inside.

Later that day, as she pondered what had happened, Fran grew unsettled. First, she'd broken a bone with her garden fork, then, minutes later, Jessie smashed her brother's leg. It was silly to think the two things were connected. Yet Fran couldn't shake the feeling that they were.

Chapter 2

Leo Walker stayed in hospital for two whole weeks. The only person who visited him was Mrs Walker. The twins weren't allowed to go with her, but they tried to sneak into the back of the motorcar when their grandmother wasn't looking.

"They're a pair of pests," Millie exclaimed. She was watching the twins' antics from the kitchen window one morning as Fran sat at the table, downing a glass of milk. "Who'd hit their brother so hard as to break his leg, eh? It's wickedness."

Fran explained what Evan had told her about Leo's fixation on the duke in Europe who'd been shot dead.

"That Archduke someone or other?" Millie asked. "Oh, it *was* shocking. He and his wife were killed in cold blood, and in public too. It was in the paper last week."

Fran's family didn't read the newspaper, but she agreed it sounded a grim story. "Seems a funny thing to fight about, even so," Fran replied.

"Oh, Leo's forever talking about Germany getting too powerful and Russia not liking it," Millie told her. "He thinks there's going to be a war soon, and that's scared Jessie."

"Is there?" Fran asked, surprised. "Going to be a war, I mean?"

"Back home in Ireland, maybe," Millie admitted sadly. "But not in Europe."

"So why was Jessie scared?"

Millie's face grew softer. "Ah, the wee thing loves her father. He'll have to go off and fight if there's a war. Evan's worried about it too."

"They don't *act* worried," Fran pointed out. "They act like lunatics."

"True." Millie sighed. "But I don't suppose Leo meant to upset his sister. It's just that he often struggles to say the right things."

Fran knew what that felt like. She was also still troubled by what had happened to Leo's leg. That perhaps – somehow – it was her, not Jessie, who was to blame.

*

Over the next few days, whenever she saw Jessie and Evan, Fran was tempted to ask after Leo. But the twins were always too busy throwing sticks or chasing pigeons across the lawn, or generally making noise. Anyway, Fran knew it was a silly idea, really – too silly to try to explain to anyone, especially the twins. *Fran* wasn't the person who'd whacked Leo with a cricket bat, and the bone she'd found in the potato patch probably wasn't even a human one. Yet the two things had happened just minutes apart, and this was the point she kept coming back to.

What helped Fran was keeping busy in the gardens, and in full summer there was always plenty to do. It was during the second week of Leo's hospital stay that Fran began to notice her father acting oddly. She kept catching sight of him leaning on his spade, drifting off into his own little world. It was as if her father had something on his mind too.

"What shall I do next, Dad?" Fran asked one afternoon when he seemed more distant than ever.

He pushed his cap up and blinked. "Onions, I think," her father replied. "Yes, Millie said she wanted onions."

There were two rows of onions along the back wall of the garden, their green tops withered from the sun. To the right were the potatoes. The bone was still there somewhere, lying under the soil, but Fran was determined not to think about it. She was shaking the excess mud from the last onion when something tumbled to the ground.

Fran mistook it for a white stone at first – until she caught it with her boot. The object flipped over. It wasn't a stone at all but something shaped like a tiny baby. Fran picked it up warily, with the bone incident still vivid in her head. The baby was about the length of her little finger and made of smooth white china. It was sweet, really. Fran put it in her skirt pocket to show Millie.

"Why that's a Frozen Charlotte!" Millie
laughed when she saw it. She explained the
dolls were popular little trinkets. They'd been
named after a girl who'd been too vain to dress
sensibly on a sleigh ride and had died of the
cold. It was just the sort of creepy story Millie
loved to share. "It's like the one I stir into the
cake at Christmas," Millie added, "so it's a treat
for anyone who finds it in their slice."

"Do you think it belongs to Mrs Walker, then?" Fran wanted to know.

Millie peered closer at the figure in Fran's upturned hand. "Don't think so. It looks older – probably from the last century. Finder's keepers, that's what I say."

Fran smiled.

"It's a bit chipped, though," Millie pointed out.

Fran didn't mind that the Frozen Charlotte wasn't perfect. She was just glad it wasn't another bone.

*

Later that afternoon, Fran's mother made an announcement.

"Your father and I have something to tell you," she said to Fran as they sat down for their tea.

Fran had sensed something was going on the moment she'd come indoors. The table had been laid with her mother's special tablecloth, the one with butterflies sewn along the edges, which normally only came out for birthdays. There was cake too, as well as bread and butter. Fran's mother was wearing a pretty blouse tucked into a rather tight skirt. It was odd for Fran to see her mother without her pinny.

"It's not something bad, is it?" Fran asked, feeling worried.

Her mother laughed, catching her father's eye across the table. "I hope not, love."

Fran relaxed a little.

"You see, the thing is, love," her mother started, paused, then said in a rush, "it seems you're going to have a little brother or sister soon."

"What do you think of that, eh?" Fran's father asked.

Fran frowned at her plate. Her mother was having a *baby*? Wasn't it a bit late for that? There'd be such an age gap between the baby and Fran. A baby would be so small. So noisy. Fran would be expected to play with a brother or sister, to look after them, to actually *like* them. She felt a pang of pity for Leo Walker and thought how hard it must be for him, with the twins.

Fran's mother and father were waiting for her to say something. Her father was smiling proudly. Fran couldn't remember the last time he'd looked so relieved, so happy. This was probably why he'd seemed distant before in the garden.

"Well?" Fran's mother asked gently. "Is it a bit of a shock, love?"

"What? No," Fran replied, and sat up in her seat. "I'm fine, really. I'm pleased."

"You'll be a wonderful big sister, I know you will," her mother said. She took Fran's hand and squeezed it fondly. Her father stood up and kissed the top of her head.

They were lovely, both of her parents. Fran knew she should be thrilled.

But it wasn't just about the baby – at least, not the one growing in her mother's belly. What troubled Fran was the china figure in her skirt pocket. Twice recently Fran had discovered something in the garden. And those *somethings* had predicted future events. First Leo's broken leg and now her mother having a baby. Even if they *were* just coincidences, it was spooky. Fran dreaded to think what she might find next.

Chapter 3

When Leo returned to Longbarrow House, the doctor's orders were for him to have complete bed rest. Fran guessed the twins had been finally allowed to see him; from the giggles wafting down from an open upstairs window, it sounded as if they were keeping their elder brother entertained.

In the kitchens, Millie made up food trays for Leo – not just at mealtimes but heaving plates of sandwiches and cake in between. After two weeks of hospital food, Leo's appetite was back

with a vengeance. At least that's what Millie
told Fran, who pretended not to be interested.

"He keeps asking for the newspaper," Millie
confided. "But Mrs Walker says he should read
something more wholesome."

Fran remembered the argument between
Leo and Jessie. "He's still on about a war, then?"
she asked.

Millie nodded. "He goes on about lots of
things, does Leo. Gets obsessed. Doesn't know
when to stop. He's what you might call *intense*."

Another reason to keep out of Leo Walker's
way, Fran reminded herself.

*

Fran did her best to avoid Leo. Yet one
afternoon she stumbled across him while on
an errand for her father. Leo was alone on the

lower lawn, sitting in a wicker bath chair with a blanket tucked around his knees. Fran was about to turn heel and run. But it was too late: Leo had spotted her.

"Haven't seen my blasted siblings, have you?" he called.

Fran shook her head: no, she hadn't. She wondered why Leo was such a long way from the house. It wasn't exactly warm out here. The morning had been bright, but the sky was rapidly clouding over and a cool wind stirred the trees.

"The twins brought me outside for some fresh air, then abandoned me," Leo said.

"Oh." Fran felt herself becoming tongue-tied. "Umm ... oh dear."

"There are supposed to be peace talks, you know, to calm things down a bit in Europe," Leo went on. "I only mentioned it once, but Jessie told me to shut up and Evan said I was a bore. That was the last I saw of them."

To Fran's surprise, Leo seemed almost as shy as she was. He could hardly meet her eye, and his hands kept smoothing down the already neat blanket.

"I've been sitting here for over an hour," Leo confessed.

He looked thinner than when she'd last seen him – paler and quieter too. Leo really should be indoors on a sofa before a fire, Fran thought. It wouldn't be right to walk off and leave him. Besides, Fran hadn't yet shaken off the sense that it was *her* fault that he'd broken his leg. If she'd dug the potato patch just a bit to the left, she'd never have hit that bone.

"I'll take you back to the house," Fran decided.

Before Leo could object, she stepped behind
the bath chair and gripped the handles.

Fran pushed. The chair didn't move. She
pushed harder until she was leaning almost at a
diagonal.

"The brake!" Leo cried, pointing at a lever
beside the right-hand wheel.

There was a clunk of metal as Fran freed the lever and the bath chair lurched forwards. Even with the brake off, it wasn't an easy thing to move. The wheels dragged across the grass, and the lawn was full of small bumps and dips that made Leo wince.

"Ouch! Oh! I'm sorry!" Fran kept saying.

"You're a fat lot more careful than the twins," Leo assured her.

By the time they reached the edge of the lawn, Fran was sweating and breathing hard. Her arm muscles burned from the effort of pushing. Thankfully, the bath-chair wheels ran more smoothly out on the main drive. Fran moved faster.

"Is your leg getting better?" she asked Leo. Talking to the back of his head felt easier than speaking to his face, somehow.

"Bearable," he replied. "It's the boredom that's worse – being stuck in this stupid chair all the time."

"Do you read books?" Fran said. If she had a broken leg, she'd do nothing *but* read for weeks on end.

"Newspapers," Leo told her. "When I can get my hands on them."

Fran frowned. "Oh."

"And my two stupid siblings who are meant to be looking after me are about as much help as—"

"Two left feet?" Fran offered.

Leo turned around to face her, looking confused.

"Never mind," Fran muttered, feeling awkward again.

She was glad when the trees thinned and the handsome grey-stone front of Longbarrow House came into view.

"I'll fetch your grandmother," Fran said, leaving the chair at the bottom of the front steps.

"Brake!" Leo reminded her.

Scowling, Fran kicked the lever downwards.

She hesitated for a moment, unsure whether to go to the staff entrance at the back of the house like she usually did or knock on the main door. Before she had decided, the front doors flew open.

"There you are, Leo!" Mrs Walker cried, rushing down the steps. "Where on earth have you been? I was about to send out a search party!"

Even in a panic, Mrs Walker still managed to look flawless. Today she was wearing a blue-striped day dress with buttons all down one side. Fran had seen a similar outfit in the fashion magazines Millie read.

"Blame Evan and Jessie," Leo replied.

"They left him, Mrs Walker," Fran explained. "By himself on the lawn."

Mrs Walker rolled her eyes. "Whatever are we to do with them? Those children are impossible!"

A couple of housemaids appeared to help Leo out of the chair and back inside. Fran remembered the errand she still had to do and turned to go, but Mrs Walker called her back.

"Thank you for bringing Leo home, my dear," she said.

"I only did what anyone would've done," Fran insisted.

"Though not his own siblings, clearly." Mrs Walker sighed wearily. "I was foolish to think the twins could be trusted to look after him properly. I wonder, might you do it instead?"

"*Me?*" Fran gulped in surprise.

"There are very few people Leo lets push him in that chair, believe me," Mrs Walker confided. "He doesn't make new friends readily, but I can see he's already quite at ease with you. And the poor mite is going out of his mind with boredom."

"He did mention that," Fran admitted.

"You could explore the place while the good weather holds. It'd be far more fun than him recovering indoors, don't you think?" Mrs Walker added.

"So you'd like *me* to look after Leo?" Fran repeated. The thought of spending every afternoon with Leo Walker made her feel confused. She could think of a hundred excuses why she couldn't do it – she would be busy helping her father, her mother. She didn't much like other children. And glancing at the empty bath chair – with its two big side wheels and a smaller one at the front – Fran knew what a devil it was to push.

"I don't think so—" Fran began to say.

Mrs Walker interrupted, "I'm counting on you, my dear, to take Leo's mind off things. Stop him terrifying his poor siblings with his talk of war."

She said it gently but firmly, so Fran knew she didn't really have a choice.

"I think the gardens might make a nice change for Leo from the political situation in Europe, don't you?" Mrs Walker added.

Fran, who knew far more about gardens than politics, supposed she was right.

Chapter 4

The next afternoon, Fran found herself staring at the back of Leo Walker's head once again.

"Be back for tea at four," Mrs Walker said to them, tapping her wristwatch. She was very punctual about mealtimes.

Fran grimaced: four o'clock was two hours away – two long, awkward hours looking after a boy she had nothing in common with.

"Where would you like to go?" Fran asked Leo, trying to sound more eager than she felt.

The gardens stretched out in all directions – acres of lawn, flowerbeds, ornamental box hedges, cedar trees. Further still to the north was a beech grove and beyond that a meadow. There was so much to explore here at Longbarrow, Fran hardly knew where to start.

"I don't really mind," Leo said. He seemed as uncomfortable as Fran was with his grandmother's plan and kept fidgeting with his jacket sleeves.

"Let's look at the roses," Fran decided. The muscles in her arms were still sore from yesterday, and there were some lovely rose beds just behind the house, which wasn't far.

"I'm not really interested in gardens," Leo admitted.

"What *are* you interested in, then?" Fran asked, but right away wished she hadn't. Mrs Walker had warned her to keep Leo off the subject of the news.

"The name of this house for a start," Leo said. "You know what a long barrow is, don't you?"

"Like a wheelbarrow, only longer?" Fran suggested.

She was grateful that Leo didn't laugh.

"It's an ancient burial site," he replied. "For warriors or people of high status. Grandmother claims the house got its name from the local river, but I'm not so certain."

"Because that's called the River Barrow, not *Long* Barrow?" Fran guessed.

"Partly. And this place, these grounds – they feel very old, don't you think?"

Fran knew what Leo meant: the gardens did feel strange sometimes, especially at dusk, when everything seemed to hold its breath. But surely her father would have mentioned a burial site if there was one here – he knew the estate inside out.

"We should look for it," Leo decided, sounding excited. "It'll be far more fun than staring at flowers."

Fran's mind spun back to the broken bone. Perhaps there were bodies lying underneath the neat rows of potatoes her father had planted. She shuddered.

"I don't think we should," Fran warned. "Not if there are dead bodies."

"You won't be able to *see* any skeletons," Leo assured her. "It'll just be a boring old mound covered in grass, I bet you."

Fran sighed. Mrs Walker was counting on her to keep Leo busy. And since the gardens weren't holding his attention, she found herself agreeing to his idea. She had to admit, it did sound intriguing.

*

Every afternoon for the next two weeks, Leo
and Fran searched for a burial site that might
or might not exist. From two o'clock until four,
Fran pushed, pulled and dragged Leo and his
bath chair around the Longbarrow Estate. It
was exhausting work that blistered her hands
something awful. Yet it surprised Fran how
much she enjoyed herself. Not that she and Leo
were friends, exactly. Most of the time they
didn't even speak to each other. But being quiet
with another person was different from being
quiet on your own, Fran realised.

They walked across lawns, down cinder
paths, through groves of beech trees. They
toured the meadows, scoured hedgerows, walked
to the boundary walls and back again. They
found little parts of the estate Fran had never
seen before, but nothing that looked remotely
like a burial mound.

By Thursday afternoon, the weather had turned. The air was still and thick, the sun only dim in a flat grey sky that promised thunder. It was too hot for doing anything. They'd been walking just a few minutes when Fran insisted they stop for a breather in the shade of a huge yew hedge. Sweat was dripping into her eyes. All she could think about was the homemade lemonade that would be waiting for them back at the house.

Fran had already guessed Leo wasn't ready to give up yet. He was tracing their route from the past two weeks in an imaginary map across his legs. "We went here," he explained. "Here. Even all the way up here. So I don't understand how we've not found it."

Fran flopped down beside him on the grass. "We've tried our best. Ouch!" She sat up again. "Something just hit me!"

Behind them, a rustling came from the hedge. A giggle. Something small and green whizzed past Fran's head. A crab apple landed in Leo's lap.

"Jessie! Evan!" Leo roared. Forgetting his leg, he leapt up, then fell back into his chair, red faced.

The giggling got louder. More tiny apples flew from the hedge. Fran scrambled to her feet, and one hit her on the ear.

"Owww!" she yelped. "That ruddy hurt!"

Jessie and Evan broke cover. They ran away across the lawn in a whirl of arms and legs and laughter.

"I'll be glad when they go back to their school," Leo muttered.

"Hmmm," Fran agreed. But no twins meant no Leo, and she was getting to rather like him being around.

*

That night, thunder and lightning kept everyone awake. The next day began cool and wet, with heavy rain making the trees drip and the ground squelch. It was still raining after lunch. There wasn't much chance they'd be able to search the gardens today, but Fran went over to the house anyway and found Leo in the library.

"What a waste of an afternoon," Leo said crossly. "We should be outside searching, not sitting about in here."

Privately, Fran was glad of a day off from pushing the wretched bath chair. She was also beginning to doubt Leo's theory about the burial site.

"Perhaps the house *is* named after the river," Fran suggested.

"I don't think so," Leo replied. "There's an atmosphere in this place, as if something has happened in the past. Can't you feel it?"

Fran frowned. "Ghosts, do you mean?"

"Maybe. Do you believe in ghosts?" Leo asked.

Fran chewed her lip. She thought of the bone again, and the odd little china doll. The two incidents still worried her, despite nothing more turning up in the garden.

"Why don't we play cards till the rain stops?" Fran said, keen to change the subject.

Reluctantly, Leo agreed. Next, they had to find a pack of cards. Fran pulled out desk drawers and rifled through piles of books, but they weren't in any of the likely places.

"Try that box." Leo directed her to a large oak chest on top of the desk.

The box wouldn't open on her first try. On her second attempt Fran noticed a piece of paper stuck in the gap between the desk and the wall. It was dusty, cobwebby, as if it'd been there for a long time.

"There's a bit of paper down here," she told Leo.

Leo sat forward with interest. "Can you reach it?"

The space was narrow, but Fran managed to wriggle her hand in. She pulled out a crumpled, yellowed folded piece of paper about the size of a chessboard. The paper fell open as she brushed off the cobwebs.

It was a map of Longbarrow Estate. Fran recognised some of the names written on it: "Hardy's Grove", "the back lane" and "Barrow Cottage", her home – a small square near the main gates. She passed the map to Leo.

He took it eagerly, his eyes skittering across the paper.

"Look!" Leo jabbed his finger at a spot on the map, close to where they'd been yesterday. There was a symbol shaped like a ring of dashes. Beneath it, in tiny old-fashioned writing, were the words "burial chamber".

Fran gnawed her lip, uneasy all over again. Just when they were about to give up the search, she'd found the one thing that might help them. It was yet another strange coincidence, she was certain of it. Longbarrow was still playing tricks on her.

But it was too late to explain the earlier coincidences to Leo now, when Mrs Walker was calling them for tea.

Chapter 5

Fran wanted to see the burial chamber as much as Leo did, despite her sense of dread. So, when the rain eased, they agreed to meet later that evening. By the time Fran had washed up the supper things, her parents were already dozing in their chairs. The clock on the kitchen mantelpiece showed quarter past seven. Fran put a hand on her stomach to calm herself – ten minutes until she had to leave.

She felt nervous. Excited. Nervous again.

Unable to sit still, Fran pulled on her shoes and tidied her hair. As she opened the door, her mother called out drowsily, "Don't go too far, love, it's a bit dimpsy out there."

"I won't," Fran replied. "Just need a bit of fresh air."

"Meeting a sweetheart are you, eh?" her mother teased.

Fran felt her face turn beetroot red.

"I've got a headache, that's all!" Fran cried, and hurried from the house.

Outside the light was already fading. Rain was forecast again for tomorrow, and the sky was so heavy it almost seemed to press down on the world.

Fran was still bristling at her mother's comment as she ran down the path that led to the back of Longbarrow House and the kitchens.

It was here that she'd meet Leo – with Millie's assistance.

"I'm glad you two are getting along," Millie had said when Fran asked for her help. Millie wasn't sure why they had to hide their plan from Mrs Walker, but relented, saying, "If it'll keep Leo's nose out of the evening papers, then why not?"

At the kitchens, Leo was already waiting in the doorway. Millie stood behind him, her arms folded across her chest.

"You've got an hour before Mrs Walker notices you're gone," Millie warned before slipping back inside.

Fran rubbed her hands together. "Are you ready?" she asked Leo.

"You're late," Leo said.

Fran glanced at his wristwatch. "By a minute."

"That's still late," Leo answered.

She was learning that Leo spoke sharply when he was nervous. He didn't intend to be as rude as he sounded.

"Well, I'm here now," Fran told him.

Leo shook out the map, spreading it across his knees. Fran tried to read the lines and squiggles, the names written sideways, but she couldn't get her bearings.

"Show me where the big house is," Fran demanded.

Leo pointed to Longbarrow House, drawn as a T shape. The long stalk part was the rear of the house, which backed onto the courtyard in front of them.

"And the burial site?" Fran asked.

Leo's finger landed higher up the paper. "Here."

*

After a brisk five-minute walk, they were back at the yew hedge where they'd been the day before. It looked different in the gloomy light – strange and unsettling.

"It's that way," Leo said, and pointed beyond the hedge to where the path narrowed. "Another five or so minutes, I think, and we should find it."

They set off again. Fran felt tense. For once she was glad to be pushing the chair, because it gave her something to focus on. But after five, then ten minutes of walking, she was beginning to think they were lost, when they took a sudden right turn. It brought them out on the cinder path that ran alongside the wall surrounding the kitchen gardens. Fran began to get her bearings again. But when the wall ended, the path took them on through a stretch of land she didn't recognise. These past couple of weeks they'd searched the gardens from top to bottom, but she'd never seen this part before. She stopped, confused.

"How did we miss finding this?" Fran asked.

"I don't know," Leo admitted. "It's like it's just appeared. As if by magic or something."

Fran shivered.

"Maybe it is magic," she agreed.

Leo looked at her. "I *was* joking, Fran."

"I wasn't," she muttered under her breath, and started pushing the bath chair again.

The gardens quickly became open fields. There'd clearly not been much need for gardening out here, since the grass was being grazed by sheep. The land was rougher, with a wild feel to it, as if the countryside was bursting in past the railings.

"That's got to be it," Leo said, pointing to a spot about fifty yards in front of them. Fran's

gaze followed his finger. "There. The grassy mound. Can you see it?"

She nodded. Swallowed.

The mound was about halfway across the field. It wasn't much taller than the dung heap around the back of Mrs Walker's stable yard. Yet Fran couldn't take her eyes off it. A tugging sensation seemed to be pulling her straight towards it.

They set off across the rough grass, with the chair bumping, lurching, tipping dangerously sideways. When they reached the mound, Fran stamped the chair's brake on, stood back and stared.

"So *this* is a burial mound," she murmured.

"It's called a barrow," Leo corrected her. "Hence the name Longbarrow, as I've said all along."

"How old is it?" Fran asked, suspecting Leo would know.

"Looks Anglo-Saxon to me. So, it's from sometime between the fifth and eleventh centuries, before William the Conqueror got here."

Fran nodded. She knew about William the Conqueror because they'd studied the Norman Invasion in school.

From this angle, the mound looked like nothing more than a bump in the ground. A few loose stones lay scattered at the base. Here and there on its slope were patches where the grass didn't grow. It was a bit of a disappointment, really. Yet Fran felt oddly alert, as if something was about to happen, though she didn't know what.

"There should be a door," Leo said, seeming frustrated. "A main door for taking the corpses in and a spirit door for their souls to use to escape."

Corpses. Spirits.

Fran's pulse quickened. Before Leo could say more, she was scrambling up the slope.

"Hey, where are you going?" Leo cried.

"To look," Fran told him.

At the top of the mound, the view was magnificent. Fran was able to see the whole valley: the village houses with lamps already twinkling at their windows, the wooded slopes beyond and the River Barrow spooling across the middle like a dark thread. It was a view she'd only ever glimpsed from their attic window at home, and Fran could well understand why someone might choose to be buried here.

"Well?" Leo called to her. "*Is there a doorway round there?*"

She'd forgotten she was meant to be looking for one.

At her feet, the ground dropped away sharply. The soil was thin and stony. The soles of her boots slipped over it, showering grit onto the brambles that tangled round the bottom of the mound. Even if there was a door down there, Fran didn't fancy her chances of finding it.

A strange sensation came over Fran then. Like a hand tugging at her sleeve, urging her not to leave. Something stirred beneath her feet. A tremble. A vibration. There was a smell too – of dirt and leather – so strong suddenly she could almost taste it.

Below her, as if buffeted by a wind she couldn't feel, the brambles swayed apart. She caught sight of a hole in the side of the mound, as small and narrow as a pantry window. Its edges were framed by slabs of stone, which gave it the look of an entrance, a way in or a way out.

This, Fran realised, was the spirit door.

Chapter 6

Fran slid down the mound in a flurry of earth. Brambles tore at her clothes and hair as she went, yet she managed to reach the bottom in one piece. The entrance looked even smaller down here. The framing stones were patchy with moss. There was no actual door to open. Even crawling on her belly, Fran didn't think she'd get inside. And she wasn't sure she wanted to.

"Fran?" Leo called. His voice sounded distant. "What are you doing?"

As she crouched there, hesitating, she caught another waft of leather and felt a tug on her sleeve. The tugging grew insistent, as if someone was demanding that Fran look inside.

"Give me a minute!" she called to Leo.

Fran shook back her hair. She didn't feel scared, exactly – more as if every nerve, every muscle was pulled tight. On her hands and knees, she eased her head inside the entrance, remembering to keep her mouth firmly shut in case of spiders. As she edged forwards, it quickly grew too dark to see. The air smelled damp, like compost. Fran's shoulders then hips brushed against the sides of what seemed to be a tunnel. Painful little stones ground into her elbows. If she lifted her head a fraction too much it hit the roof. A rush of fear filled her. The last thing Fran wanted was to get stuck in this place.

Mercifully, up ahead the darkness thinned. . Cracks in the roof let in what remained of the

daylight as thin as a pencil, but it was enough
to see the tunnel open up all around her. Fran
took a deep breath, feeling slightly calmer. Her
eyes grew used to the murky light and she
saw marks on the wall – scratches, symbols.
The ground beneath her started tilting gently
downhill, which made crawling easier. She
shuffled on.

The skeleton, when she saw it, almost didn't
look real. It lay across the passage, just a few

feet ahead. Fran froze. The bones lay on the ground, level with her face. She didn't dare move closer, yet she couldn't tear her eyes away. She'd never seen a dead body before, let alone one this old. The legs were straight, with the arm nearest to Fran flung across the rib cage. Something glinted inside the skeleton's torso – a sword blade or a dagger. There were other objects lying nearby – another sword, a spear, a shield. And a skull, with its jaw open from its last blood-chilling scream.

Panic took hold of Fran. Her mind spun with thoughts of broken bones and china babies. This place was another sign, she was sure of it. It terrified her to think what this old skeleton might be warning her of, because it certainly wouldn't be something good. Fran's heart was beating so fast she felt light-headed. She needed to get out. Even in this part, the tunnel was too tight to turn around in, so she shuffled backwards as fast as she could.

Outside again, Fran gulped the cool evening air. Once her head felt clearer, she brushed the worst of the mud from her knees and hurried back to Leo. He was hunched forward in the bath chair, looking very fed up.

"I thought you'd abandoned me too," he remarked.

"Sorry," Fran said. She stood in front of him, rubbing her arms. She felt cold and exhausted. "Leo, there *is* an entrance round the other side, like you said there would be."

His face brightened. "There is? A proper spirit door? Oh I say! Take me round there, will you?"

"I'd rather not, actually," Fran replied.

"But I'd really like to see it," Leo pressed. "Please, it won't take us long. We've come all this way out here. It's not fair that you've seen it and I haven't."

Fran gritted her teeth – she knew he wasn't going to give up.

"Look, I went inside," she confessed. "Properly inside ... and I saw a skeleton."

Leo's eyebrows shot up. "How on earth did you manage that?"

"I crawled in," Fran explained. "There was a passage that got bigger, and a bit of light coming in from a crack in the roof. And the skeleton was there, in front of me, surrounded by weapons."

"By weapons," Leo repeated.

He doesn't believe me, Fran thought sadly. Then she realised, from the twisting of Leo's hands, that he was trying to contain his excitement.

"An ancient burial chamber with treasure inside, right here on Grandmother's land!" Leo gasped. "And to think we only set out to prove the house's name. What an incredible discovery!"

Fran folded her arms. Now it was her turn to be stubborn.

"Why won't you go back inside?" Leo demanded.

"Because I ..." Fran trailed off. She wasn't sure how to tell him about the strange things she kept finding in the gardens. It was going to take some explaining, but she knew she ought to try.

Fran swallowed hard.

"Just before your leg broke, I found a bone in the potato patch," she said. "I cracked it by mistake with my garden fork. Then, a week or so after that, amongst the onions, I came across a tiny china doll. And then, just hours later, my mother told me she was having a baby."

Leo looked confused. "What has this got to do with the burial chamber?"

"Strange stuff keeps happening," Fran insisted. "It's like the garden is trying to tell me things, and then today, when we were about to give up, we found that map ... If we go poking around in that tomb any more, then I'm afraid—"

The expression on Leo's face made her stop. He was staring at a spot beyond her. Fran hesitated, wondering if she'd sounded a bit daft in the head. But as she turned to see what had caught Leo's attention, her breath stopped.

A man.

Two men.

A whole group of them appeared around the side of the burial mound.

Fran blinked. No, it was the dusk playing tricks on her eyes, she told herself. They weren't men, they were trees. Except trees didn't move, and these were coming towards them.

There had to be twenty or thirty at least, marching two abreast. All were wearing grubby tunics, cloaks and boots laced to the knee. Just like the costumes people wore at the village fair, Fran thought. But this wasn't a game. These men looked like warriors going into battle. They carried weapons – proper mud-splattered shields and swords. Some wore helmets that covered the tops of their faces. Every single one of them looked frighteningly fierce.

Fran's stomach heaved in terror. She stepped back. The men kept coming. They were only a few feet away now, marching right towards Fran and Leo. Yet the strangest thing was the men weren't making any noise. No clanking of metal, no thudding boots on grass. No chants or songs to encourage nervous feet. If Fran had shut her eyes, she might not even have noticed them but for the sudden drop in temperature and the strong smell of leather and earth. All she could hear was her own heartbeat, which drummed in her ears.

Fran was sure she was going to die of fear right there. And if that didn't kill her, then one of the warriors would do the job with his sword. Or trample her and Leo to the ground.

Fran braced herself. As she squeezed her eyes tight shut, a strange sensation hit her. Like a hiccup caught in her chest. As fast as it came, it went again. What followed was a rush of pain: tiny jabs that stung and needled.

When Fran dared open her eyes, the men had gone. In the distance, across the field, she saw the last of the soldiers disappearing like mist between the trees. The only sign they'd ever been there was the flattened path they'd tramped over the grass.

"Did that really just happen?" Leo asked. He put his head in his hands and gripped fistfuls of hair.

"I ... I ... I think so," Fran replied. "Who were they?"

Leo let go of his hair. It stuck up oddly all over his head.

"Soldiers," Leo said. "Anglo-Saxon I'd guess, judging by their weapons."

"But they can't be real!" Fran cried.

"Of course they're not," Leo replied. "Haven't you ever heard stories about ghost armies?"

"You think that's what we've just seen, then? Ghosts?"

"Probably," Leo said. "I read that they appear as a warning – that a war or some other national emergency is about to happen."

"You do know how ridiculous that sounds, don't you?" she muttered, and yet, when she'd seen the skeleton inside the mound, hadn't she feared something similar herself?

Fran felt tired and bewildered. Too many strange things had happened here at Longbarrow over the past few weeks. She didn't want to think about what the men – the soldiers – might mean, and what would happen next. She wanted to believe that they'd dreamt it all. Fallen asleep. For there to be a simple explanation.

"Put that map away and let's go home," Fran decided.

Leo nodded. "Good idea."

Chapter 7

That weekend, Fran's father bought a newspaper for the first time ever. She hovered at his shoulder to read it, learning that peace talks in Europe had failed before they'd even started. Germany had declared war on Russia and was threatening to invade Belgium.

Leo was right, Fran thought miserably, there was going to be some sort of conflict in Europe. He was also right about the soldiers they'd seen at the burial mound. The ghost army had been a warning.

As she lay in bed that night, Fran overheard her father talking about signing up to fight if Britain got drawn in to the war. Fran felt the air leave her chest all at once. She caught herself agreeing with Jessie Walker: it *would* be terrifying if a person you loved went to war. She hoped with all her might it wouldn't come to that.

In an attempt to take her mind off war, she thought of tomorrow instead. Every August Bank Holiday Monday Mrs Walker held a garden party for the locals. It was a noisy, busy affair that left the lawn horribly pock-marked by ladies' heeled shoes and would take Fran's father ages to restore. Normally, Fran had mixed feelings about the party. This year she was glad of the distraction.

*

The day of Mrs Walker's garden party dawned breezy and cool. All morning, Fran helped Millie by cutting sandwiches and dusting icing sugar over her perfect scones. When that was done, Fran picked sweet peas from the garden and put a bunch on each of the tables set outside for the guests.

By mid-afternoon, the lawn of Longbarrow House was so busy with flapping tablecloths and fluttering summer dresses it was as if a whole swarm of butterflies had descended on the grass. Fran was with her parents, sitting cross-legged on a blanket under the trees. Her father, in his best pinstriped suit, seemed relaxed, almost handsome. Her mother had let out her skirt seams and was very obviously pregnant. The pair of them looked radiant. If there was a war, Fran thought with a pang, she'd remember this afternoon.

"Fetch us another scone, love." Her mother held out her plate to Fran.

Glad of an errand, Fran weaved between the crowds to where the food was laid out on trestle tables. Evan and Jessie Walker were there, helping themselves to cucumber sandwiches. They looked as quaint as dolls – Jessie in a dress of white lace, Evan in a sailor suit – yet were both attacking the food like wild animals. Fran hoped she could get her mother's scone and slip away before the twins saw her, but she had no such luck.

"Hewwwoooo, Frannie!" Jessie boomed.

A mouthful of Jessie's half-chewed sandwich fell onto the grass. Evan started giggling. Within seconds the pair of them were in fits.

"Jessie, Evan," Fran said, and dipped her head in their direction.

"Come and play cricket with us, Frannie," Evan begged. "You can play, can't you?"

"I don't expect she can," Jessie answered for her. "Frannie's too busy being Leo's nursemaid to play games with us."

That set them off into more hoots of laughter.

"My name is Frances," Fran told them, very coolly. "Or Fran, if I like you. *If.*"

Jessie and Evan stopped laughing.

"Gosh," Jessie whispered. "Terribly sorry."

"We didn't mean anything unpleasant," Evan muttered.

"And," Fran added, getting into her stride, "looking after Leo has been pretty decent, actually. If my new brother or sister turns out anything like him, I'll be happy."

"That's because Leo likes you," Jessie said sulkily.

"If you spent less time annoying him and more time being nice, he'd like you too, I'm sure of it," Fran replied.

The twins stared at her as if she'd spoken Greek.

*

As Fran picked her way back across the grass, she spotted Leo sitting at the last table on the lawn, wearing a smart linen suit. Mrs Walker was with him, shooing wasps off her jam scone.

"I hear you made a discovery, my dear," Mrs Walker called out as Fran drew near.

"I did?" Fran asked, and shot Leo a worried glance.

Mrs Walker nodded. "One of Old Rex's bones, so my grandson tells me."

It took a moment for Fran to realise what Mrs Walker was talking about. Old Rex was her last dog. He'd been big and white, covered in black spots, and bred to run alongside carriages before he'd become too fat.

Mrs Walker looked misty-eyed. "Old Rex always did like burying bones in the potato patch, the dear boy," she said.

Fran's mouth dropped.

Mrs Walker must be talking about the bone Fran had been so sure was a human one – the one she'd broken and was convinced had caused Leo's accident.

"You're sure it was Old Rex's?" Fran pressed her.

"Why yes." Mrs Walker frowned. "Who else's would it be?"

Fran let out a long breath. She felt rather stupid.

"Well." Mrs Walker stood up. "I'll leave you young people to chat."

When she'd gone, Fran sank into Mrs Walker's empty seat. She felt a mix of relief and bafflement. So, the bone had belonged to Mrs Walker's old dog. But that didn't explain the little china doll, the map and the ghost army.

"Do you think the other things were coincidences, then?" Fran asked Leo.

"Maybe." Leo shrugged. "I've been thinking about it a lot these past couple of days."

"So finding the Frozen Charlotte wasn't a prediction?" Fran challenged.

"Your mother is having a baby," he replied. "She'd still be having one whether or not you found a china doll."

"But the timing of it—"

"Was probably a coincidence," Leo cut in. "And the fact that you weren't looking very hard."

Fran scowled at Leo. "I look," she snapped. "I notice things."

"Do you? The *really* little things?" Leo asked. "I guessed your mother was pregnant the day we arrived here for the summer. She looked different – thick-waisted and tired."

"You noticed *that*?" Fran was taken aback.

"As for the map," Leo went on. "I'm sure someone would've found it sooner or later."

"But *we* did," Fran pointed out. "It helped us find what we were looking for. Or do you think the ghost army was a coincidence now too?"

Leo seemed suddenly less certain.

"I hope so," he replied.

Fran, who'd always wanted a simple explanation for all these strange happenings, hoped so too.

*

Early Tuesday morning, Fran was on her way to the kitchens when she saw Leo out on the front steps of the house. The morning paper rested in his lap. He'd got hold of it before Mrs Walker could whisk it away.

"I'll drop these tomatoes off for Millie, then we can go for a walk," Fran suggested to Leo.

She was in a good mood. How could there be anything odd about Longbarrow House on such a bright, sparkling morning? The gardens looked as beautiful today as they'd ever been. Even the pock-marked lawn still seemed lush and green. At home, Fran's father hadn't mentioned joining the army again. Her mother was blossoming. Fran was even beginning to look forward to having a baby brother or sister. After weeks of feeling fearful, she decided it was time to cheer up.

When Fran saw the headline on the newspaper in Leo's lap, it was like walking into a wall.

"It can't be!" she gasped. "No, no, no, it can't be!"

But it was. There in bold letters, right across the front page, it said: "GREAT BRITAIN DECLARES WAR ON GERMANY".

Thoughts crowded Fran's brain. Everyone had treated Leo like an odd eccentric, but he had been right all along. Fran's father would now join the army. Jessie and Evan would be upset about their father going to war too. Fran shook her head. None of it seemed real when she was standing on the front steps of Longbarrow House, listening to the blackbirds sing.

Fran gripped the bath-chair handles and tried to push Leo across the lawn. The brake was on, and as she went to release it, Leo put his hand very gently on her arm.

"Hang on, speedy," he said. "You're thinking about the ghost soldiers, aren't you?"

"Aren't you?" Fran cried.

"A bit," he admitted. "I mean, we *did* see them, didn't we?"

Fran shivered, remembering the leather and dirt smell. "We definitely did."

"Yesterday, I thought it was all coincidences," Leo said. "I didn't honestly believe we'd really get to the point of an all-out war, yet it's happened. And I can't stop thinking that those soldiers were a prediction."

Leo twisted in his seat to look at Fran – properly this time – meeting her eye. "What do you think? Do you still believe in predictions?"

"I don't know," she replied.

There were things she could never have predicted, like her friendship with Leo. At the start of the summer, she hadn't thought much of friendship – she'd preferred her own company. Yet in a strange, fated way, some good had come from Leo's accident. The two of them had been thrown together and become rather decent friends.

"My mother's coming home from Paris," Leo said as they made their way towards the kitchens. "She's taking us out of boarding school so we can all be together. We'll be going to our local schools from now on."

"That'll help Jessie," Fran replied. "She needs her family. It'll be hard for all of you, knowing your dad's going to war."

As Fran said it, she thought of her own situation, which wasn't so very different. She needed her parents. She needed friends. A baby was coming – a brother or a sister. Her little family was growing. Perhaps there was a link between all these things. Perhaps her beloved garden had foreseen the future. Maybe it was telling her this: that difficult times are better faced together.

Behind the story

In *The Ghost Garden*, nobody wants to listen when Leo tries to warn them about events that are happening in Europe in the summer of 1914, but at the end of the story we learn that his worst fears have come true. Britain has declared war on Germany, and it is likely that Leo's father and Fran's will have to go off and fight.

One of the most important steps on the road to war was the assassination that Leo and Jessie argue about. Archduke Franz Ferdinand, the heir to the throne of Austria-Hungary was shot on 28 June 1914. He was killed by a Serbian man, Gavrilo Princip, and this led Austria-Hungary to declare war on Serbia.

At this time, Europe was divided into two large sets of countries. One set was the Allies – the British Empire, France, Belgium and Russia. The Central Powers were the other set, including Germany, Austria-Hungary, Bulgaria and Turkey. Once Austria-Hungary had declared war, the other countries were also drawn in. When Germany invaded Belgium on 4 August 1914, Britain felt it had no choice to but to defend its ally, and so war was declared between Britain and Germany.

At first everyone thought the war would be over quickly – by Christmas that year. But in fact it would drag on for four long years and cause the deaths of over 16 million people. New weapons, vehicles and methods of warfare were used for the first time, leading to horrific numbers of casualties.

Peace was finally declared on 11 November 1918, with the Allies being declared the victors. But tensions would continue to simmer in Europe over the next decades and another terrible war would come in 1939.

Our books are tested
for children and young people by
children and young people.

Thanks to everyone who consulted on
a manuscript for their time and effort in
helping us to make our books better
for our readers.